THE
POOL PARTY
FROM THE
BLACK LAGOON®

Get more monster-sized laughs from

The Black Lagoon®

THE
POOL PARTY
FROM THE
BLACK LAGOON®

NICE CATCH.

by Mike Thaler

Illustrated by Jared Lee

SCHOLASTIC INC.

For Teresa & Jerry Weydert
Always in the swim!
—M.T.

To Tom and Sara Davidson
—J.L.

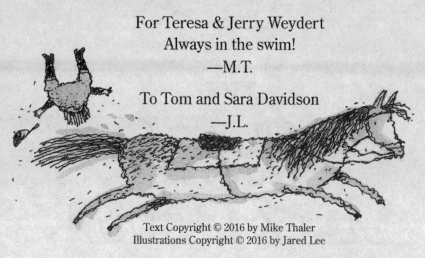

Text Copyright © 2016 by Mike Thaler
Illustrations Copyright © 2016 by Jared Lee

ISBN 978-0-545-85073-5

12   19 20

Printed in the U.S.A.   40
First printing 2016

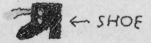 ← SHOE

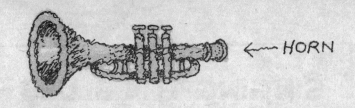

← HORN

CONTENTS

← SHOEHORN

CHAPTER 1

SINGING THE BLUES

I can't swim. I hate water. Actually, I'm afraid of it. I even wear water wings in the bathtub. I don't even like going in a car pool.

I'VE GOT FLEAS.

So when Penny announces in class that she is going to have a pool party in two weeks—I am not happy. Not happy at all!

All the other kids are thrilled. They can't wait. I can wait. I *am* a weight. I will just sink to the bottom and turn blue. I am already beginning to turn blue.

"What's the matter, Hubie?" asks Penny as she hands me a mermaid invitation.

"Nothing," I answer. "Nothing at all."

10

CHAPTER 2
DIFFERENT STROKES

On the bus ride home from school, nobody can talk about anything else.

"I can swim across the pool," says Penny.

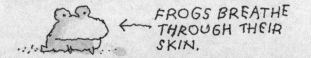

FROGS BREATHE THROUGH THEIR SKIN.

"I can swim across *underwater*!" brags Eric.

"I can jump in," says Doris.

"I can *dive in*," brags Eric.

YIPPEE!

"I can do a cannonball," says Freddy.

"I can do a *flip*," brags Eric.

"I can hold my breath for a minute," says Penny.

  COOTIE HIDING IN THE SAND

"I can hold my breath for *two minutes*," brags Eric.

"Oh yeah?" says Penny.

"Oh yeah!" boasts Eric, puffing out his chest.

FULL OF HOT AIR

"Well, let's just see *who* can hold their breath the longest," challenges Penny.

"Okay," blusters Eric.

Penny starts counting, "One, two, three," and everyone takes deep breaths.

I do, too. My cheeks puff up, my eyes bulge out, and after twenty seconds I start turning blue. I make a noise like a leaky tire. Everyone looks at me, but they all keep holding their breath.

BLUE BECOMES YOU.

Luckily, my stop comes. I run off the bus. When I look back, they are all still holding their breath and staring at me out the bus window.

CHAPTER 3
OUT OF THE FRYING PAN

When I get home, I run to my room and dive into bed. Mom comes in.

"What's the matter, Hubie?"

"Penny's having a pool party," I sigh.

"How nice," Mom says.

"No, it's *not* nice, it's horrible!"

"Weren't you invited?"

CLOSE YOUR LEGS.

21

CHAPTER 4
DEEP DESPAIR

The next day Mom takes me to the public pool. It is deep. It is dark. It is wet. I don't see any shark fins, but there are lots of kids splashing around.

Besides the water, the *public* part bothers me. What if the kids have diseases? And what if they don't take baths? Real diseases and germs. Germs float. This is not a place I want to be. It's like a

garbage can with a diving board. Mom says it's perfectly clean. Every day they put in chlorine. Chlorine kills germs—in fact it kills just about anything. Oh great—I hope it doesn't kill me!

← GERM

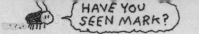 

CHAPTER 5
I WANT MY MOMMY

The instructor comes over.

"I'm Mr. Sharky," he announces while grabbing my hand.

"This is Hubie," Mom says. "He can't swim."

"No problem," Mr. Sharky says, still shaking my hand. "We'll whip him into an Olympic champion in no time."

"I'll leave him in your hands," Mom says, and walks away.

"Let's get started," he says. "Go to the locker room."

28

Oh great. Is he going to lock me up? Are there kids chained to the walls? I think.

YOU'RE JUST SMELLING THE CHLORINE.

MR. SHARKY, I'M FEELING FAINT.

He gives me a key on an elastic band. I'm supposed to wear it on my wrist . . . I guess it's so they can identify the body.

"Put on your bathing suit and we'll get started."

CHAPTER 6
A CHANGE FOR THE WORST

BURRR...

The key opens a locker. I'm #34. I don't have a name anymore . . . I'm just #34. I take off my clothes. My warm, dry clothes. I put on my bathing suit. It's not really a suit—like with a tie and a jacket. It's more like a wide rubber band. It's chilly in the locker room . . . and wet. The floor is wet. The pool is coming to get me!

BURRR...

There is a sign on the wall that says:

TAKE A SHOWER BEFORE ENTERING THE POOL.

I can do that. I walk into the shower room. It's not like the shower at my house. There are lots of showers all in a row. I pick one. At first it's too hot. Then it's too cold. I'm not going to sing in this shower.

CHAPTER 7
A SINKING FEELING

I head toward the pool. I'm already soaked and haven't even been in the water yet. There's a long hallway full of signs.

POOL RULES:
NO RUNNING
NO DIVING
NO SPLASHING
NO SHOUTING

I wish it said NO SWIMMING.

I finally come to the pool. Everyone's running, diving, splashing, and shouting. I guess the rules are just for the hall.

Mr. Sharky comes over.

"Hubie, we're doing great so far."

Oh yeah, he's dressed and dry, and I'm wet and shivering.

"Knock, knock," he smiles.

"Who's there?" My teeth chatter.

"Hubie."

"Hubie, who?"

"One day Hubie a great swimmer!"

Oh great . . . I'm standing at the edge of disaster with a stand-up comic wearing a tank top. He blows the whistle.

"Okay, Hubie, into the pool."

CHAPTER 8
IN THE SWIM!

I put water wings on my arms and my legs. After standing on the first step for half an hour, I finally go in up to my knees. It's not so bad ... so I go in up to my belly button. Then I hold on to the side and learn to kick. Then

I let go of the side and see that I can float. Then I float and kick all the way across the shallow end. I'm swimming!

Z

HE MUST BE AN OLYMPIAN.

39

The next day I put my head in the water. The day after that, I open my eyes underwater. Hey, this is cool!

By the end of the week, I have jumped into the deep end and am swimming across the pool. Mr. Sharky gives me a certificate that says I'M A MINNOW. Okay, when are the Olympics? I'm ready for a pool party.

MINNOW ⟶

41

After my lesson, I look in the locker room mirror. I'm too wimpy to be an Olympian. I'm too wimpy to go to a pool party. Well, at least now I can swim.

43

CHAPTER 9
KEEP THE CHANGE

That night I see an ad on television.

"Are you WIMPY? Are your muscles PUNY? Are you embarrassed to be seen in a bathing suit? If your answers are yes, yes, yes . . . you need the Mr. Muscles Super Galactic Flex Belt! Within one week you can become a BIONIC, BICEPS-BULGING MR. AMERICA . . ."

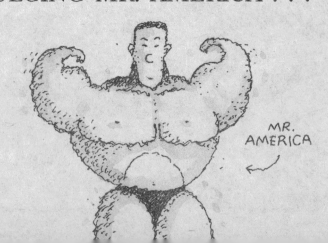

MR.
AMERICA

"Instantly go from FLAB to FAB! For only $19.95 we will send you one Super Galactic Flex Belt and in one week you will be the envy of all your friends. But wait . . . if you call this toll-free number RIGHT NOW, you will receive not one but TWO Super Galactic Flex Belts! Become a hero at the beach or pool . . ."

"I'm dialing! I'm dialing!"

CHAPTER 10
NOT FOR MINNOWS

That night I have a dream. I'm being shot to the moon by a giant slingshot. *BOING!*

As I fly closer and closer, I see that the moon is not solid. It's a giant swimming pool! I realize

that I've never learned how to high-dive. That's the next lesson. I wake up falling out of bed.

CHAPTER 11

THE HOME STRETCH

It takes two days for the box to arrive. It has a big picture of Mr. Muscles on it. I eagerly open the box and two large rubber bands fall out. There is also a one-page flyer showing different exercises.

53

I start right away. I still have three days before the pool party. It's hard work and by Friday all I wind up with is one broken

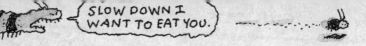

rubber band. I guess that's why they give you two? Instead of Mr. Muscles, I look more like Mr. Wuss-cles.

CHAPTER 12
TAN IN A CAN

Looking in the mirror, I realize that I'm pretty pale. Not bronzed at all. But there's no time left to sit in the sun. Besides, I get sunburned just watching TV.

RABBIT
← EARS

THROW IT TO THIRD BASE!

CAN'T WE TAKE A BREAK?

Then I see an ad for "Insta-Glow—Quick and Easy Spray-on Tan. No fuss, no muss, no bother. Insta-Glow. Your ticket to macho!"

I empty my piggy bank and rush down to the store to grab the last can. Then I hurry home to spray my way to awesome. I eagerly shake the can and press the nozzle . . . *whoosh, whoosh, whoosh!* When the mist settles, I'm not bronze . . . I'm orange. Oh well, at least I can swim.

RUSHING
TO THE
← STORE

59

CHAPTER 13
PARTY HARDY

Mom drives me over to Penny's house. I've never been here before. It's not the mansion I imagined. I get out and ring the bell. Penny's mom answers the door and tells me that all the kids are in the back. I walk around the

house to the backyard. Everyone is in their bathing suits, standing around a small, aboveground, inflatable wading pool. There is no water in it. Freddy had done a cannonball and all the water splashed out.

We have a good time anyway.
We spray one another with the
garden hose and have a water
balloon war. Penny pulls out a
slippery slide and Freddy slides

the farthest. We give Penny's dog
a bath and he splashes everyone.
Penny's mom makes hot dogs
and potato salad and Freddy eats
the most.

WATER BALLOON

After lunch, we all sit around the empty pool. I tell everyone what a great swimmer I am. And I even have a certificate to prove it.

SUPER.

SHOW THEM YOUR BICEPS.

WOW!

COOL.